HUNTING THE DADDYOSAURUS

~Teresa Bateman~

ILLUSTRATED BY Benrei Huang

ALBERT WHITMAN & COMPANY

MORTON GROVE, ILLINOIS

Library of Congress Cataloging-in-Publication Data

Bateman, Teresa.

Hunting the daddyosaurus / by Teresa Bateman; illustrated by Benrei Huang.

p. cm.

Summary: Two young dinosaurs track their father
around the house and finally tackle him in his easy chair.

ISBN 0-8075-1433-0 (hardcover)

[1. Dinosaurs — Fiction. 2. Father and child — Fiction.

3. Stories in rhyme.] I. Huang, Benrei, ill. II. Title.

PZ8.3.B314 Hu 2002 [E] — dc21 2001004316

Text copyright © 2002 by Teresa Bateman.

Illustrations copyright © 2002 by Benrei Huang.

Published in 2002 by Albert Whitman & Company,

6340 Oakton Street, Morton Grove, Illinois 60053-2723.

Published simultaneously in Canada by General Publishing, Limited, Toronto.

Printed in the United States of America.

10 9 8 7 6 5 4 3 2 1

For more information about Albert Whitman & Company,
visit our website at www.albertwhitman.com.

The design is by Scott Piehl.

For Alan, Kendall, Robert, Bill, Brian,
and, of course, my own Daddyosaurus.
—T. B.

For my courageous neighbors,
Firehouse Engine 33 and Ladder 9,
New York City.
—B. H.

The Daddyosaurus is somewhere about.

Hunka-cha, hunka-cha, rooba.

He's big and he's noisy, so better watch out!

Hunka-cha, hunka-cha, rooba.

Let's track him, attack him, and tickle him pink!
Let's give him hot cinnamon cider to drink!
He'll never escape as we shout out our chorus:
We're hunting the marvelous Daddyosaurus!

Here are his footprints — they lead to the door.
Hunka-cha, hunka-cha, rooba.
His feet are enormous, and so is his roar!
Hunka-cha, hunka-cha, rooba.

We'd better beware as we follow his tracks.
You can't be too careful, no time to relax!
He'll never escape as we shout out our chorus:
We're hunting the marvelous Daddyosaurus!

The newspaperdactyl is gone from the box.

Hunka-cha, hunka-cha, rooba.

And here are his claw covers, here are his socks!

Hunka-cha, hunka-cha, rooba.

Just look at his coat hanging up in the hall.

This dinosaur has to be ninety feet tall!

He'll never escape as we shout out our chorus:

We're hunting the marvelous Daddyosaurus!

Let's hurry upstairs. I just heard something thud.

Hunka-cha, hunka-cha, rooba.

If he's in the bathtub, the whole house will flood!

Hunka-cha, hunka-cha, rooba.

We're getting much closer, his sweatshirt is here.
It's got pizza stains and a splotch of root beer!
He'll never escape as we shout out our chorus:
We're hunting the marvelous Daddyosaurus!

He's shedding his clothes like a snake sheds its skin.
Hunka-cha, hunka-cha, rooba.
It's easy to tell from them just where he's been.
Hunka-cha, hunka-cha, rooba.

He's been in the bathroom—his towel is still wet.

The mirror is covered with dinosaur sweat!

He'll never escape as we shout out our chorus:

We're hunting the marvelous Daddyosaurus!

He's been in the office, it's easy to see.
Hunka-cha, hunka-cha, rooba.
The table is littered with dino-debris.
Hunka-cha, hunka-cha, rooba.

The kitchen! I'm sure I just heard something crunch.
(I hope he's not planning to have us for lunch!)
He'll never escape as we shout out our chorus:
We're hunting the marvelous Daddyosaurus!

Chocolate-chip cookie crumbs litter the floor.
Hunka-cha, hunka-cha, rooba.

They lead to the living room. Quick! Check the door!
Hunka-cha, hunka-cha, rooba.

We're getting much closer, I'm certain he's near—
I think that I saw him just now in the mirror!
He'll never escape as we shout out our chorus:
We're hunting the marvelous Daddyosaurus!

Quiet!

No talking!

Now tiptoe, don't giggle!

Hunka-cha, hunka-cha, rooba.

There are his toes—I saw one of them wiggle!

Hunka-cha, hunka-cha, rooba.

Let's track him, attack him, and tickle him pink!
Let's give him hot cinnamon cider to drink!

He'll never escape as we shout out our chorus:

WE'VE CAPTURED THE MARVELOUS DADDYOSAURUS!